Courtesy of Zelma Redding

**OTIS REDDING** (1941–1967) was a singer, songwriter, and producer often referred to as the King of Soul™. Known for releasing such acclaimed songs as "These Arms of Mine," "Try a Little Tenderness™," and "Respect," Redding is considered to be one of the most influential singers and songwriters of the 1960s. He was inducted into the Rock & Roll Hall of Fame and the Songwriters Hall of Fame, and received two GRAMMYs as well as a GRAMMY Lifetime Achievement Award. To learn more, visit otisredding.com.

Otis Redding was dedicated to improving the quality of life for his community through the education and empowerment of its youth. He provided scholarships and summer music programs which continued until his untimely death on December 10, 1967. Today, the mission of the Otis Redding Foundation, established in 2007 by Mrs. Zelma Redding, is to empower, enrich, and motivate all young people through programs involving music, writing, and instrumentation. To learn more, visit otisreddingfoundation.org.

**STEVE CROPPER** is an American guitarist and songwriter from Memphis, voted by *Rolling Stone* to be one of the Top 100 Guitarists of All Time. Cropper started out in a band called the Mar-Keys and was later part of Booker T. & the MG's, releasing the *Billboard* chart–topping "Green Onions" and backing numerous artists such as Otis Redding and the iconic Blues Brothers band.

**KAITLYN SHEA O'CONNOR** is an illustrator and designer hailing from Atlanta, Georgia. She combines traditional skills with digital media to create vibrant, whimsical worlds. She's a rare hybrid of dog and cat lover, an avid whistler, and she enjoys exploring the great outdoors, trying new cheeses, and cozying up in a nook with a book. O'Connor illustrated the children's picture book *We Got the Beat*, with song lyrics by Charlotte Caffey. Discover more of her work at designedbyshea.com.

"(Sittin' on) The Dock of the Bay"
Song written by Otis Redding and Steve Cropper
Courtesy of Irving Music, Inc.
Used by Permission. All Rights Reserved.

LyricPop is a children's picture book collection by LyricVerse and Akashic Books.

lyricverse

Published by Akashic Books
Song lyrics ©1967 Otis Redding and Stephen Lee Cropper
Illustrations ©2021 Kaitlyn Shea O'Connor

ISBN: 978-1-61775-850-8
Library of Congress Control Number: 2020937328
First printing

Printed in China

Akashic Books
Brooklyn, New York
Twitter: @AkashicBooks
Facebook: AkashicBooks
E-mail: info@akashicbooks.com
Website: www.akashicbooks.com

# (Sittin' on) THE Dock of the Bay

Song lyrics by **Otis Redding** and **Steve Cropper**

 illustrations by **Kaitlyn Shea O'Connor**

Sittin' in the mornin' sun

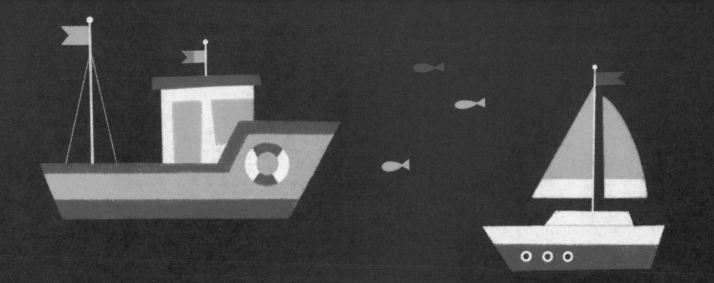

Watching the ships roll in,
Then I'll watch 'em roll away again, yeah

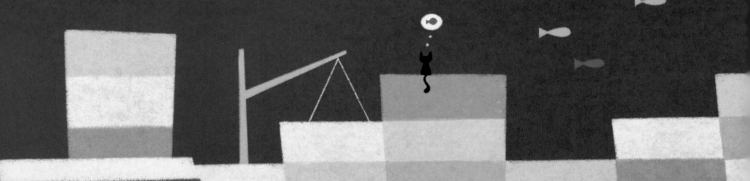

I'm sittin' on the dock of the bay

Watching the tide roll away, ooh

I'm just sittin' on the dock of the bay

Wastin' time

I left my home in Georgia

Headed for the Frisco Bay

'Cause I've had nothing to live for

It looks like nothing's gonna come my way

So, I'm just gonna sit on the dock of the bay

Watching the tide roll away, ooh

I'm sittin' on the dock of the bay

Wastin' time

Look like nothing's gonna change
Everything still remains the same

I can't do what ten people tell me to do

So I guess I'll remain the same

Sittin' here resting my bones

And this loneliness won't leave me alone

Listen: two thousand miles I roam
Just to make this dock my home

Now I'm just gonna sit at the dock of the bay
Watching the tide roll away, ooh yeah

I'm sittin' on the dock of the bay

Wastin' time

# LOOK OUT FOR THESE LyricPop TITLES

## Respect
SONG LYRICS BY OTIS REDDING • ILLUSTRATIONS BY RACHEL MOSS

*Otis Redding's classic song—as popularized by Aretha Franklin—becomes an empowering book exploring the concept of mutual respect through the eyes of a young girl.*

## The 59th Street Bridge Song (Feelin' Groovy)
SONG LYRICS BY PAUL SIMON • ILLUSTRATIONS BY KEITH HENRY BROWN

*Paul Simon's anthem to New York City is the joyful basis for this live-for-the-day children's picture book, providing a perfect vehicle to teach kids to appreciate life's little gifts.*

## African
SONG LYRICS BY PETER TOSH • ILLUSTRATIONS BY RACHEL MOSS

*A beautiful children's picture book featuring the lyrics of Peter Tosh's global classic celebrating people of African descent.*

## Don't Stop
SONG LYRICS BY CHRISTINE McVIE • ILLUSTRATIONS BY NUSHA ASHJAEE

*McVie's classic song about keeping one's chin up and rolling with life's punches is beautifully adapted to an uplifting children's book.*

## Dream Weaver
SONG LYRICS BY GARY WRIGHT • ILLUSTRATIONS BY ROB SAYEGH JR.

*Gary Wright's hit song is reimagined as a fantastical picture book to delight dreamers of all ages.*

## Good Vibrations
SONG LYRICS BY MIKE LOVE AND BRIAN WILSON • ILLUSTRATIONS BY PAUL HOPPE

*Mike Love and Brian Wilson's world-famous song, gloriously illustrated by Paul Hoppe, will bring smiles to the faces of children and parents alike.*

## Humble and Kind
SONG LYRICS BY LORI McKENNA • IILLUSTRATIONS BY KATHERINE BLACKMORE

*Award-winning songwriter Lori McKenna's iconic song—as popularized by Tim McGraw—is the perfect basis for a picture book that celebrates family and togetherness.*